"I was born in London in 1946 and grew up in a sweet shop in Essex. For several years I worked as a graphic designer, but in 1980 I decided to concentrate on writing and illustrating books for children.

My wife, Annette, and I have two grown-up children, Ben and Amanda, and we have put down roots in Suffolk.

I haven't recently counted how many books there are with my name on the cover but Percy the Park Keeper accounts for a good many of them. I'm reliably informed that they have sold more than three million copies. Hooray!

I didn't realise this when I invented Percy, but I can now see that he's very like my mum's dad, my grandpa. I even have a picture of him giving a ride to my brother and me in his old home-made wooden wheelbarrow!"

NICK BUTTERWORTH

PERCY'S FRIEND
THE OWL

NICK BUTTERWORTH

Collins

An imprint of HarperCollinsPublishers

Thanks Graham Daldry. You're a wizard.

Thanks Atholl McDonald. You're a hero!

First published in Great Britain by HarperCollins Publishers Ltd in 2001

3 5 7 9 10 8 6 4 2

ISBN: 0 00 711984 4

Text and illustrations copyright © Nick Butterworth 2001
The author asserts the moral right to be identified as the author of the work.

The HarperCollins website address is: www.**fire**and**water**.com

Printed and bound in Belgium

MY FRIEND
THE OWL

The owl is really quite clever. But, perhaps not quite as clever as she thinks she is.

She's got brilliant eyesight. But, so often, she still doesn't notice things that are right in front of her beak.

I think her mind wanders. Only the other day I asked her if she thought it was going to rain. Do you know what she answered? You'll never guess. She said, "Twenty-three." You see what I mean?

Still, the owl means well. And she'll do anything to help a friend. Anything at all. As long as she remembers...

Did I say that the owl is quite clever? Well, this was not one of her clever ideas! She thought that if she looked like an eagle, she would be able to fly like an eagle. I'm afraid she was wrong. Unless, of course, some eagles fly into things because they can't see where they're going!

THE OWL REALLY LIKES...

To be in charge. But I wouldn't
say she's bossy. I wouldn't dare!

The colour blue. She believes people would
be happier if more things were blue.

THE OWL DOESN'T LIKE...

Hats. She says that, generally speaking, they don't suit her. But she does like party hats.

Foggy weather. She says it is A Danger To Flying If Conditions Are Foggy.

I wonder if you are any better at noticing things than the owl. This mirror is very strange, it changes things. Can you see nine things that are different in the mirror's reflection? (The owl only spotted four.)

I've got lots of pictures in my photo album.

People with feathers don't usually like sticky things...

The owl tried to show the badger how to tie knots that won't come undone...

Here are some I took of my good friend, the owl.

The owl likes long words. If they don't look right, she just adds a few more letters. And why not?

The owl is very good company - especially if it's getting a bit dark!

The owl once became very
friendly with a cuckoo.
They decided to fly south
together, to somewhere
on the Isle of Wight, I
think it was.

They must have got their arrangements
mixed up. She waited on the telephone
wires for ages. Eventually, she went to sleep.

In the morning, I found her still holding
on. She hadn't noticed that she had swung
upside down. We don't talk about it.

THE OWL'S TEA TIMES TABLE

One times two is two.
Two times two is four.
Three times two is...more than that, and
Four times must be more.

Four buns would be two buns each,
If Percy came to tea.
But if the fox came with him,
We'd need another three!

But what if everybody came?
We'd need a lot, lot more.
And tables wouldn't be much use,
We'd all sit on the floor.

FAVOURITE PLACES

I know the owl likes to fly high above the tree tops on a windy day. But when I asked if that was her favourite place to be, she answered, "Not quite."

It seems that
just before take off,
standing on the top
branch of a tall tree
with the wind ruffling
your feathers...well,
the owl says there's no
better place to be.

Perhaps it's a bit like that
lovely moment just before you
take a large bite out of a fresh cheese
and pickle sandwich. Mmm! Yes, I think
I can understand what she means.

The owl lives right at the top of the big
tree house with the other animals. She has
a swing seat up there where she can sit and
watch what everybody else is doing down
below. I wouldn't say she's nosy. Just
very interested in other people.

Here she is, my friend the owl, with what looks suspiciously like my hot water bottle! I wondered what happened to it. It's been missing for a few days. It can't be hot any more, but I expect it's comfy.

THE TREE HOUSE

In this picture you'll see Percy the Park Keeper and his friends. But if you look very carefully, you can also find a balloon, a kite, a hot-water bottle, a model aeroplane, a paintbrush, a robin, a beach ball, a magpie, a yo-yo, Percy's stripy mug, a pencil, a conker, Percy's watering can, a cheese roll, a framed picture of Percy, one of Percy's gardening gloves, a model yacht, a plastic duck, a banana, and a frog. Oh, and ten ladybirds!

FREE GIANT POSTER

Nick Butterworth's new, giant picture of the tree house
in Percy's Park shows Percy and all his animal friends
in and around their tree house home. There are also
lots of things hidden in the picture. Some are easy
to find. Some are much harder!

To send off for your free poster, simply snip off
FOUR tokens, each from a different book in the
Percy the Park Keeper and his Friends series and send them
to the address below. Remember to include
your name, address and age.

Percy Poster, Children's Marketing Department,
Harper Collins Publishers, 77-85 Fulham Palace Road, London W6 8JB

Read all the stories about Percy and his animal friends...

THE OWL'S LESSON — NICK BUTTERWORTH

OWL TAKES CHARGE — NICK BUTTERWORTH

THE BADGER'S BATH — NICK BUTTERWORTH

THE LOST ACORNS — NICK BUTTERWORTH

ONE WARM FOX — NICK BUTTERWORTH

THE FOX'S HICCUPS — NICK BUTTERWORTH

THE HEDGEHOG'S BALLOON — NICK BUTTERWORTH

THE CROSS RABBIT — NICK BUTTERWORTH

AFTER THE STORM — NICK BUTTERWORTH

ONE SNOWY NIGHT — NICK BUTTERWORTH

THE RESCUE PARTY — NICK BUTTERWORTH

THE TREASURE HUNT — NICK BUTTERWORTH

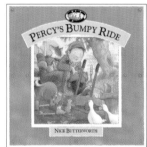

PERCY'S BUMPY RIDE — NICK BUTTERWORTH

THE SECRET PATH — NICK BUTTERWORTH

Percy the Park Keeper
Games Book

A Year with Percy
Colouring Book — NICK BUTTERWORTH

Percy the Park Keeper
1·2·3 — NICK BUTTERWORTH

Percy the Park Keeper
A·B·C — NICK BUTTERWORTH

Percy toys and videos
are also available.